# The LVE In Mending

# The L♡VE In Mending

Story & Illustrations:
MARY CATHERINE RISHCOFF

ReadersMagnet, LLC

I
dedicate
the following
book
to my sister,
KATHY A.R. EHRIG

Kathy encourages my dream of successes as children's storybook author. To that end, Kathy has greatly helped me be it with knowledge, equipment, supplies, deliveries, or just talk.

My sister, Kathy has smarts in business be it medical, shopping or else. Likewise, Kathy is college educated in both biology and psychology, which no doubt contributes to her smarts. Her smarts benefit so many persons.

I'm glad that Kathy is my sister. Over the years, Kathy has been there for me. She has "mended" me with her love. Her inspirations prompted me to write the children's storybook, The Love In Mending. With it, I honor my sister, Kathy.

Thanks ever so much!

.. Betty . . Tripper..
HOME
Sweet
HOME
.. very special relationship ..

I'm Betty. I live in a house and I own a very special dog, a Havapoo. I named my dog Tripper. He has grown to become a very special family member. Because Tripper is like family, I got him not just some, but many, many toys. We have a very special relationship now.

... toys ... stuffed animals ...

teddy bear ... Bear Sweetly

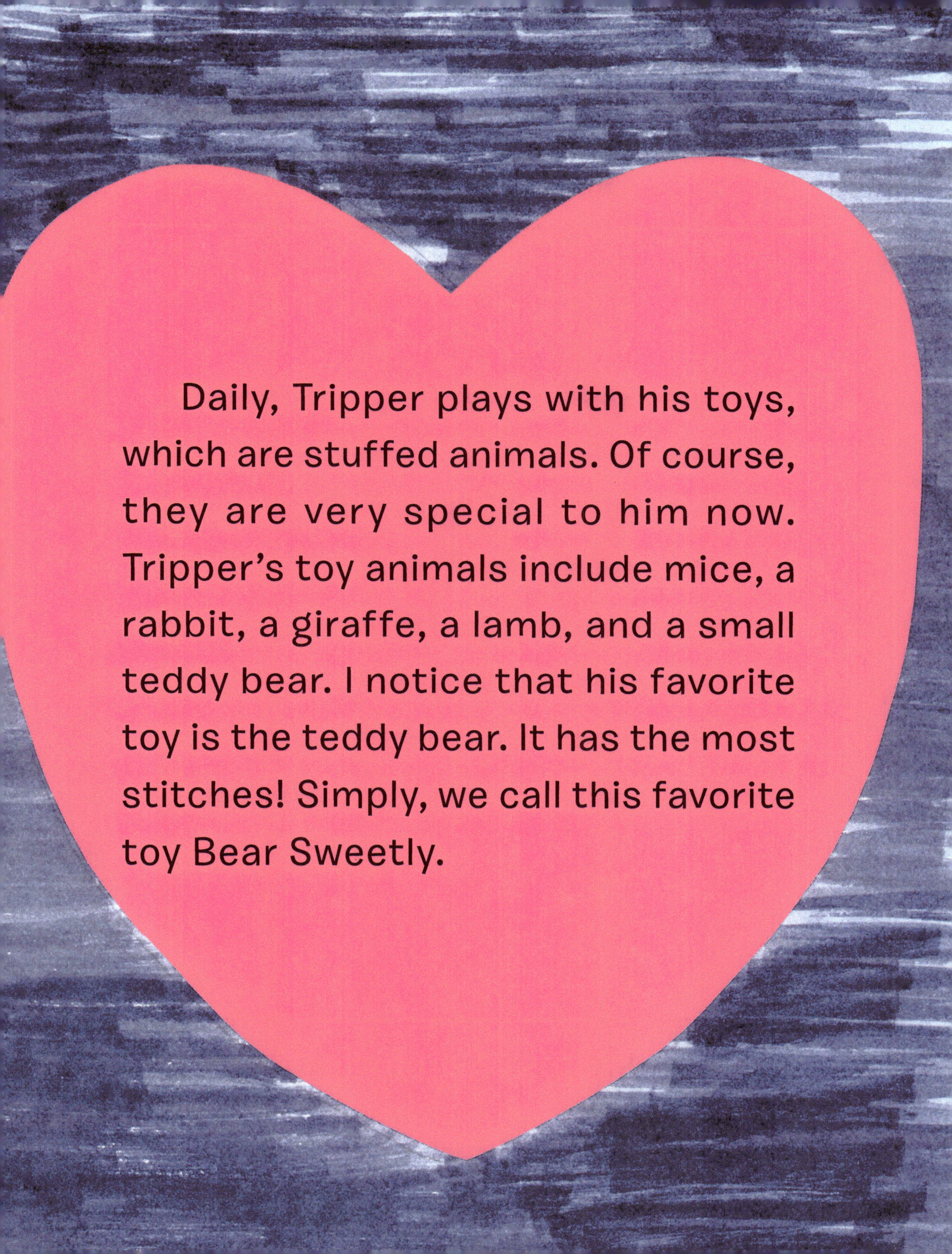

Daily, Tripper plays with his toys, which are stuffed animals. Of course, they are very special to him now. Tripper's toy animals include mice, a rabbit, a giraffe, a lamb, and a small teddy bear. I notice that his favorite toy is the teddy bear. It has the most stitches! Simply, we call this favorite toy Bear Sweetly.

... ... very special toys... ...

... sleeps ... guarding ...

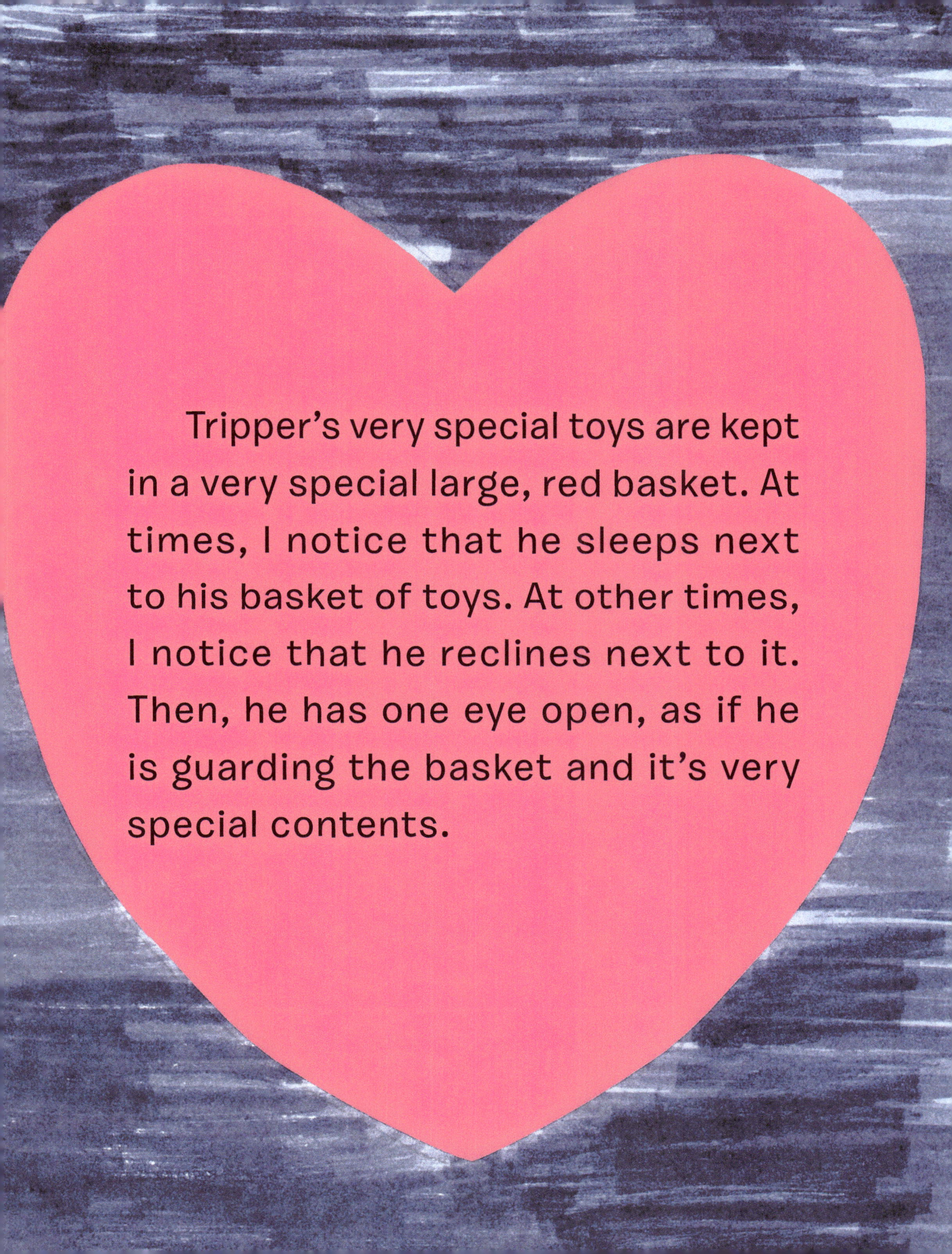

Tripper's very special toys are kept in a very special large, red basket. At times, I notice that he sleeps next to his basket of toys. At other times, I notice that he reclines next to it. Then, he has one eye open, as if he is guarding the basket and it's very special contents.

... SEW, SEW and SEW ...

... ... family heirloom ... ...

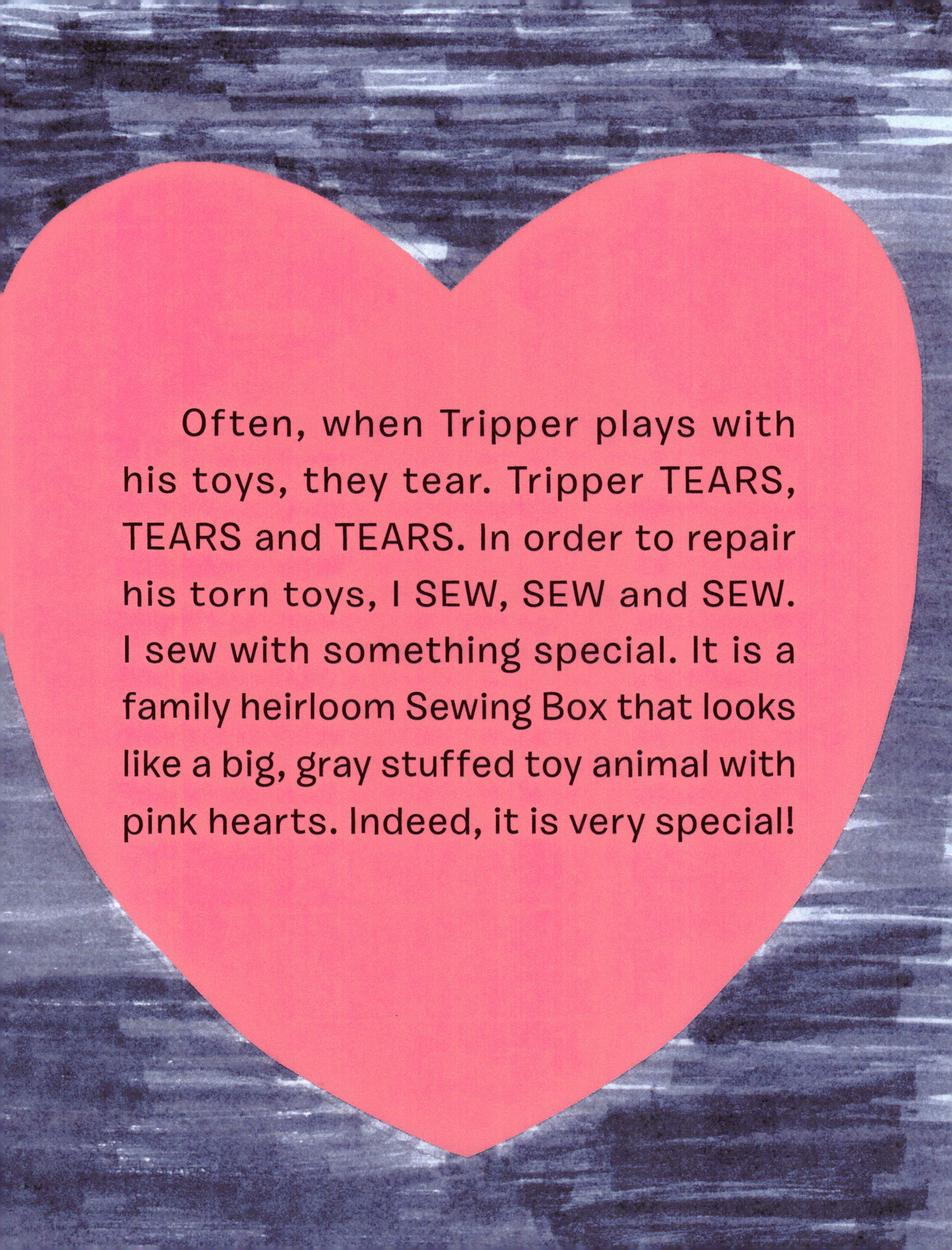

Often, when Tripper plays with his toys, they tear. Tripper TEARS, TEARS and TEARS. In order to repair his torn toys, I SEW, SEW and SEW. I sew with something special. It is a family heirloom Sewing Box that looks like a big, gray stuffed toy animal with pink hearts. Indeed, it is very special!

MEND, MEND and MEND

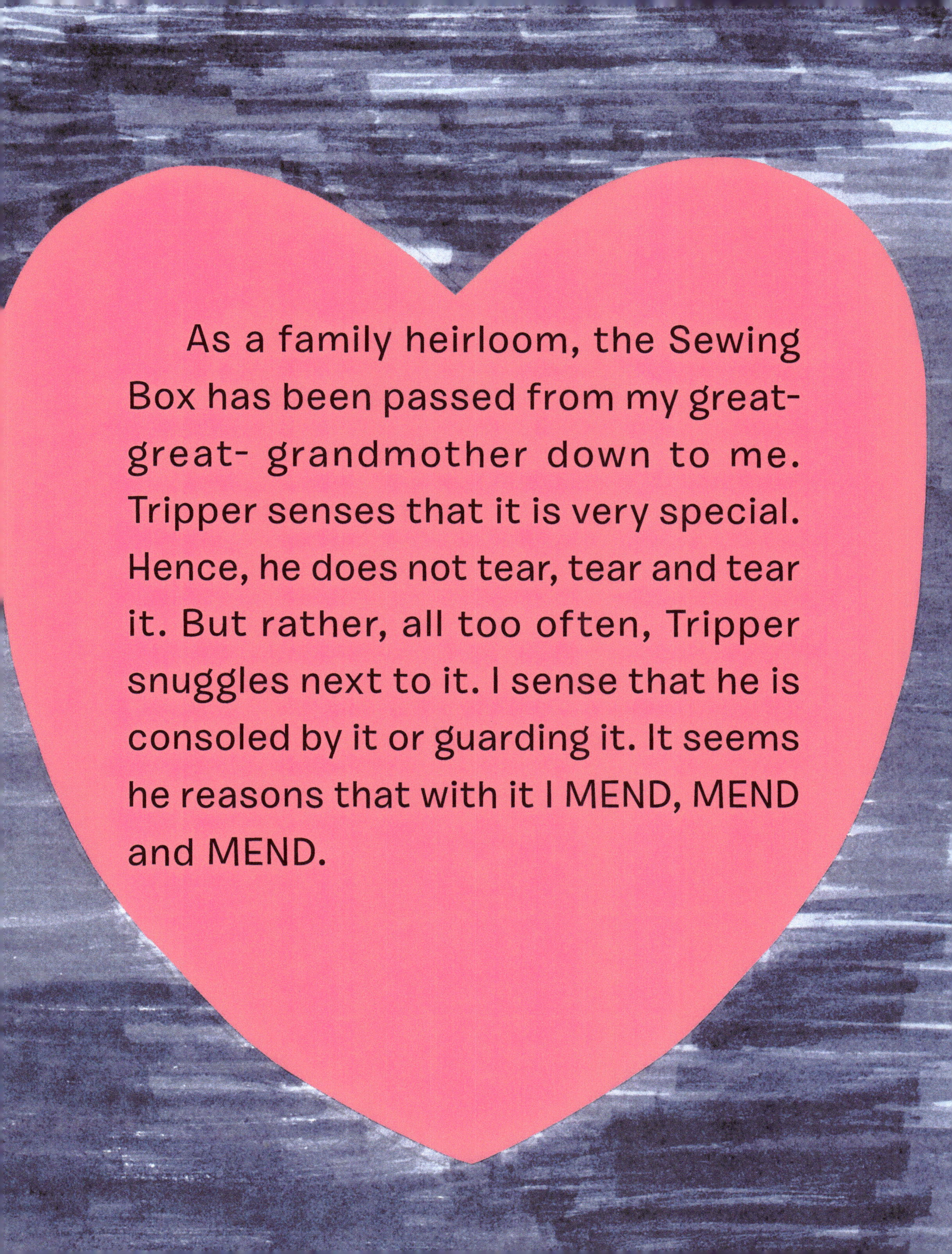

As a family heirloom, the Sewing Box has been passed from my great-great- grandmother down to me. Tripper senses that it is very special. Hence, he does not tear, tear and tear it. But rather, all too often, Tripper snuggles next to it. I sense that he is consoled by it or guarding it. It seems he reasons that with it I MEND, MEND and MEND.

... ... does not play ... ...

help Tripper ... help Tripper

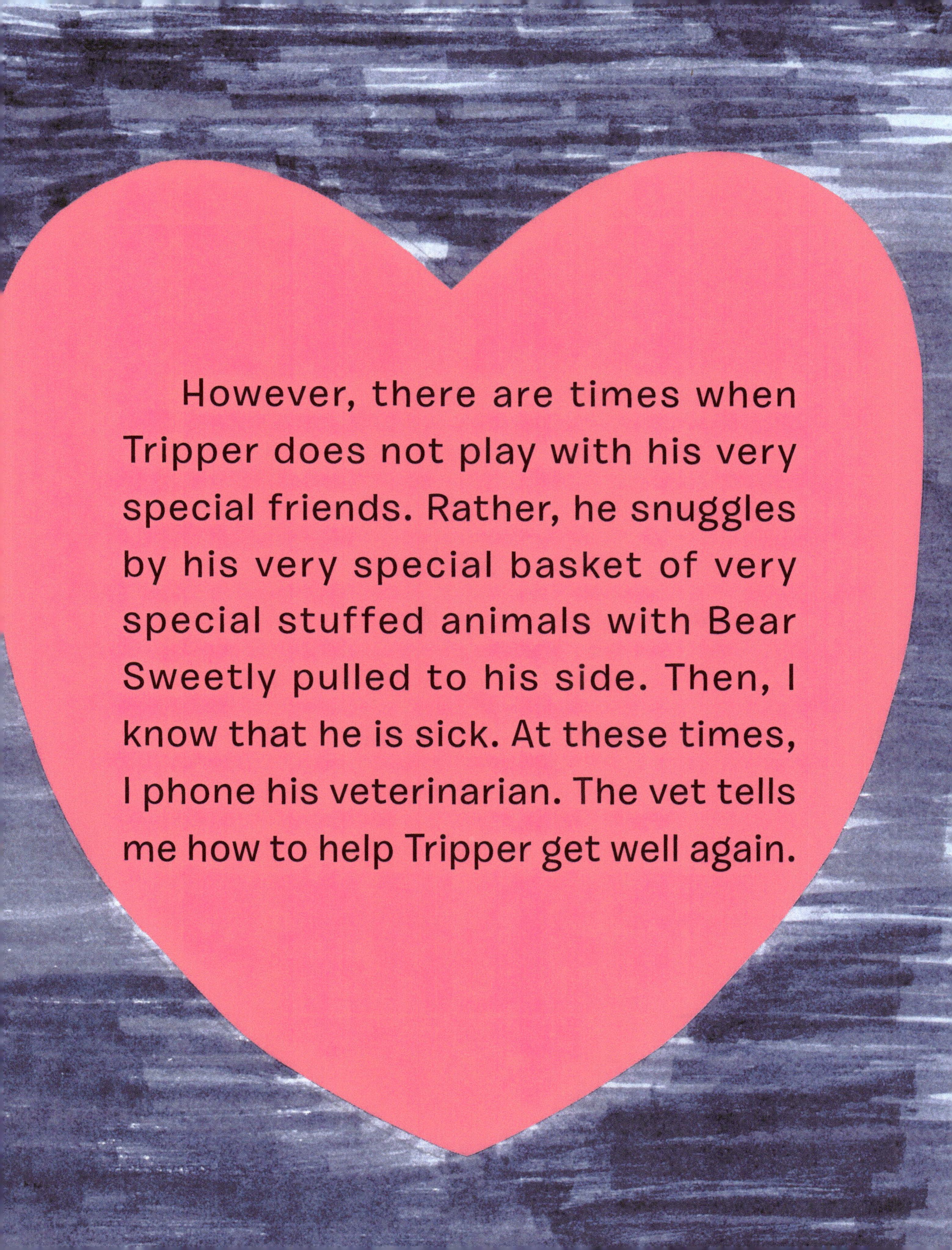

However, there are times when Tripper does not play with his very special friends. Rather, he snuggles by his very special basket of very special stuffed animals with Bear Sweetly pulled to his side. Then, I know that he is sick. At these times, I phone his veterinarian. The vet tells me how to help Tripper get well again.

… … mend Tripper … …

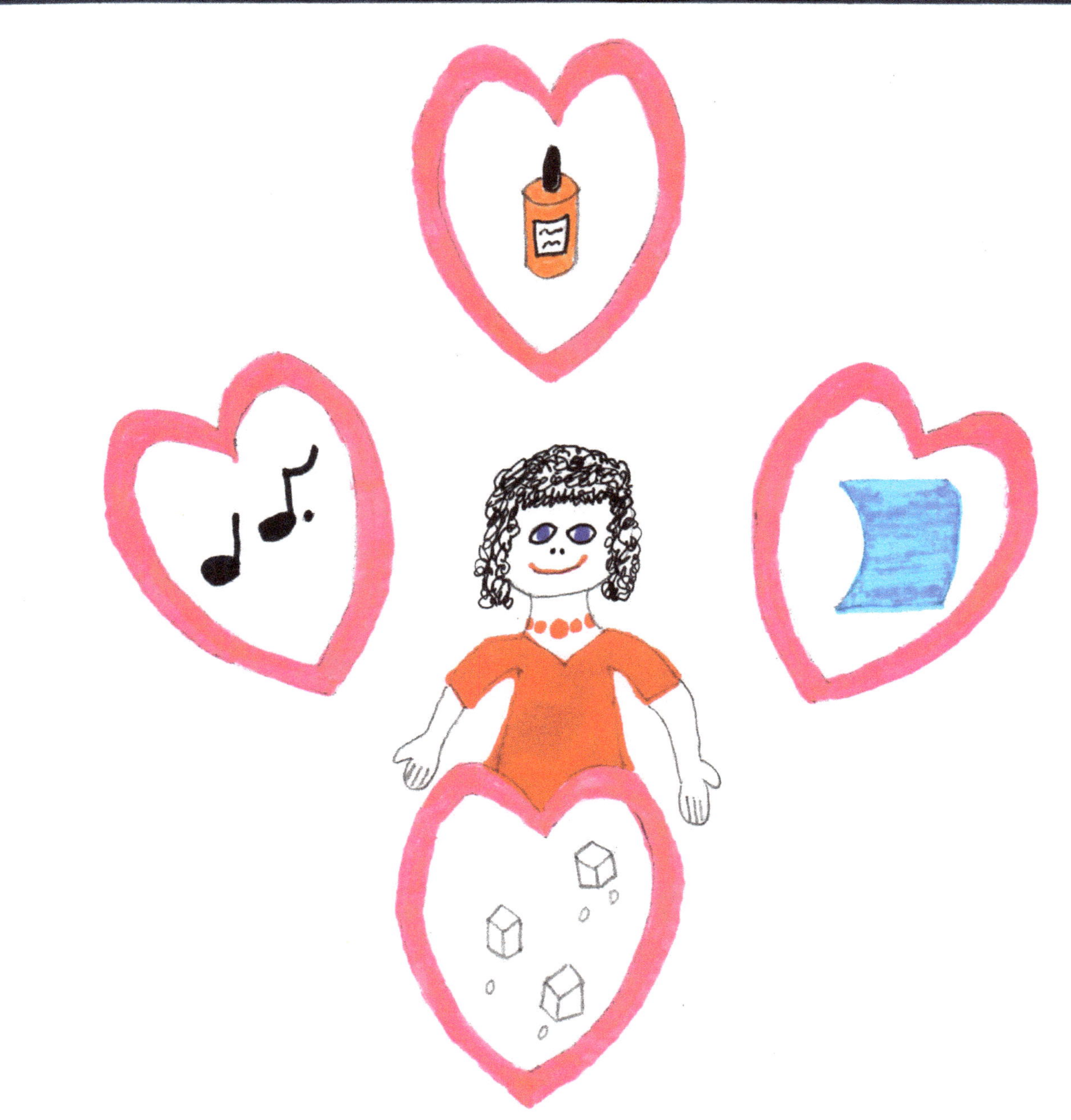

… very special Tripper …

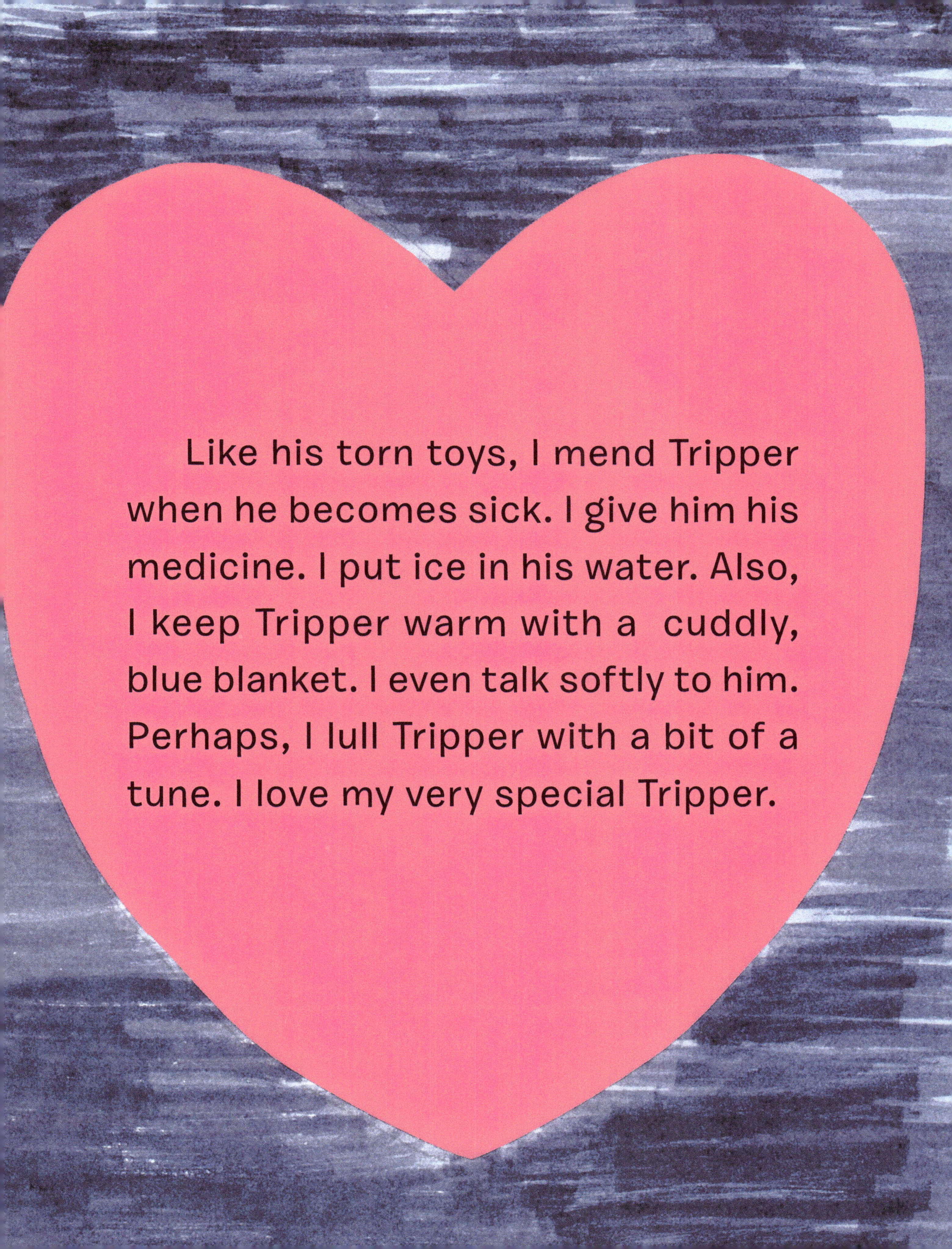

Like his torn toys, I mend Tripper when he becomes sick. I give him his medicine. I put ice in his water. Also, I keep Tripper warm with a  cuddly, blue blanket. I even talk softly to him. Perhaps, I lull Tripper with a bit of a tune. I love my very special Tripper.

... ... Tripper loves me ... ...

... I love him ... I love him ...

Tripper loves me. He loves me just as much as I love him, and maybe even more. Tripper snuggles in my lap as I rock. When snuggling with me, Tripper mends. He even keeps me company while I mend his toys. Tripper is a constant companion.

... ... pulls and tugs ... ...

... Miss Bun Bouncey ...

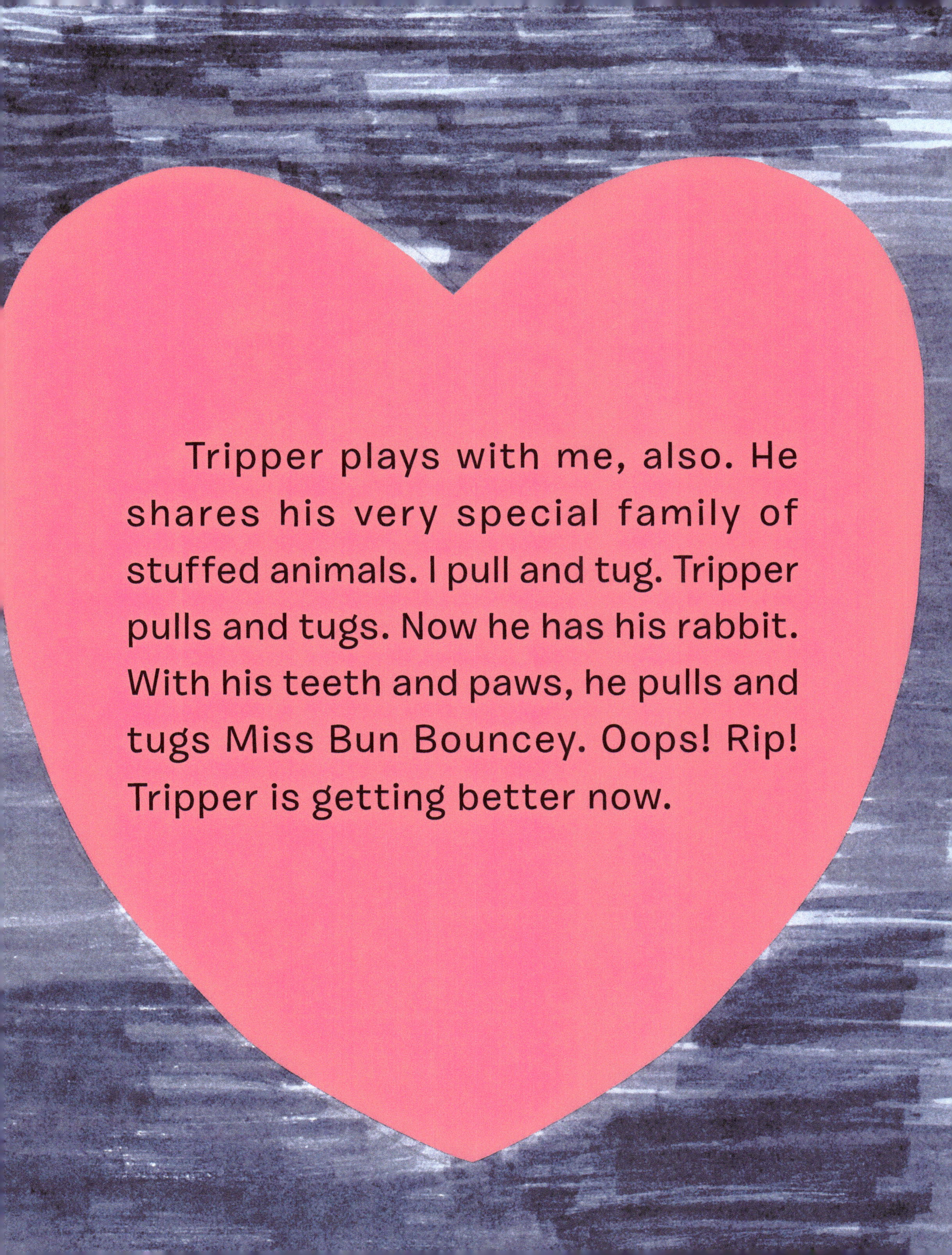
Tripper plays with me, also. He shares his very special family of stuffed animals. I pull and tug. Tripper pulls and tugs. Now he has his rabbit. With his teeth and paws, he pulls and tugs Miss Bun Bouncey. Oops! Rip! Tripper is getting better now.

… … is all well now … …

.. to the end! … to the end! ..

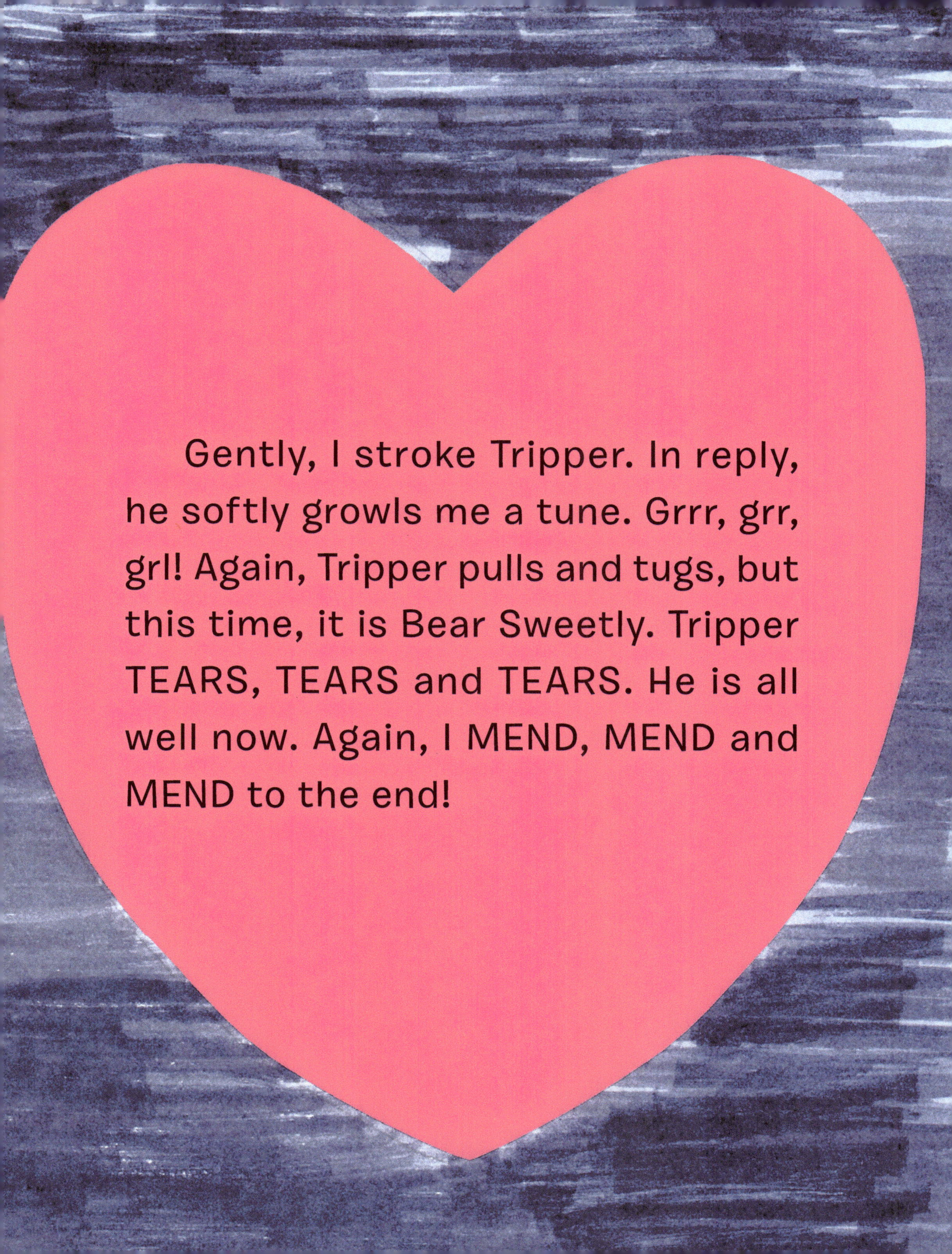
Gently, I stroke Tripper. In reply, he softly growls me a tune. Grrr, grr, grl! Again, Tripper pulls and tugs, but this time, it is Bear Sweetly. Tripper TEARS, TEARS and TEARS. He is all well now. Again, I MEND, MEND and MEND to the end!

Always!

10620 Treena Street, Suite 230
San Diego, California,
CA 92131 USA
www.readersmagnet.com
1.619.354.2643